# Vigfus the Viking

written by
## DAVID
## SACKS
## &
## BRIAN
## ROSS

*

illustrated by
## JIMMY
## HOLDER

*

Worthwhile
Books

 &

PRESENT:

www.WorthwhileChildrensBooks.com

ISBN: 978-1-60010-306-3

11 10 09 08 1 2 3 4 5

Worthwhile Books, a division of Idea and Design Works, LLC.

Editorial offices: 5080 Santa Fe Street, San Diego, CA 92109. Printed in Korea.

Worthwhile Books does not read or accept unsolicited submissions of ideas, stories, or artwork.


Jonas Books, Publisher: Howard Jonas

IDW, Chairman: Morris Berger

IDW, President: Ted Adams

IDW, Senior Graphic Artist: Robbie Robbins

Worthwhile Books, Vice President and Creative Director: Rob Kurtz

Worthwhile Books, Senior Editor: Megan Bryant

To my loves: Judy, Moshe, Sara, Mendy, and Talia ✳ **D.S.**

For my parents; my wife, Susan; and my girls, Cohava, Tirtza, & Temima, with love ✳ **B.R.**

For my girls, Suzanne, Maddi, and Charlotte ✳ **J.H.**

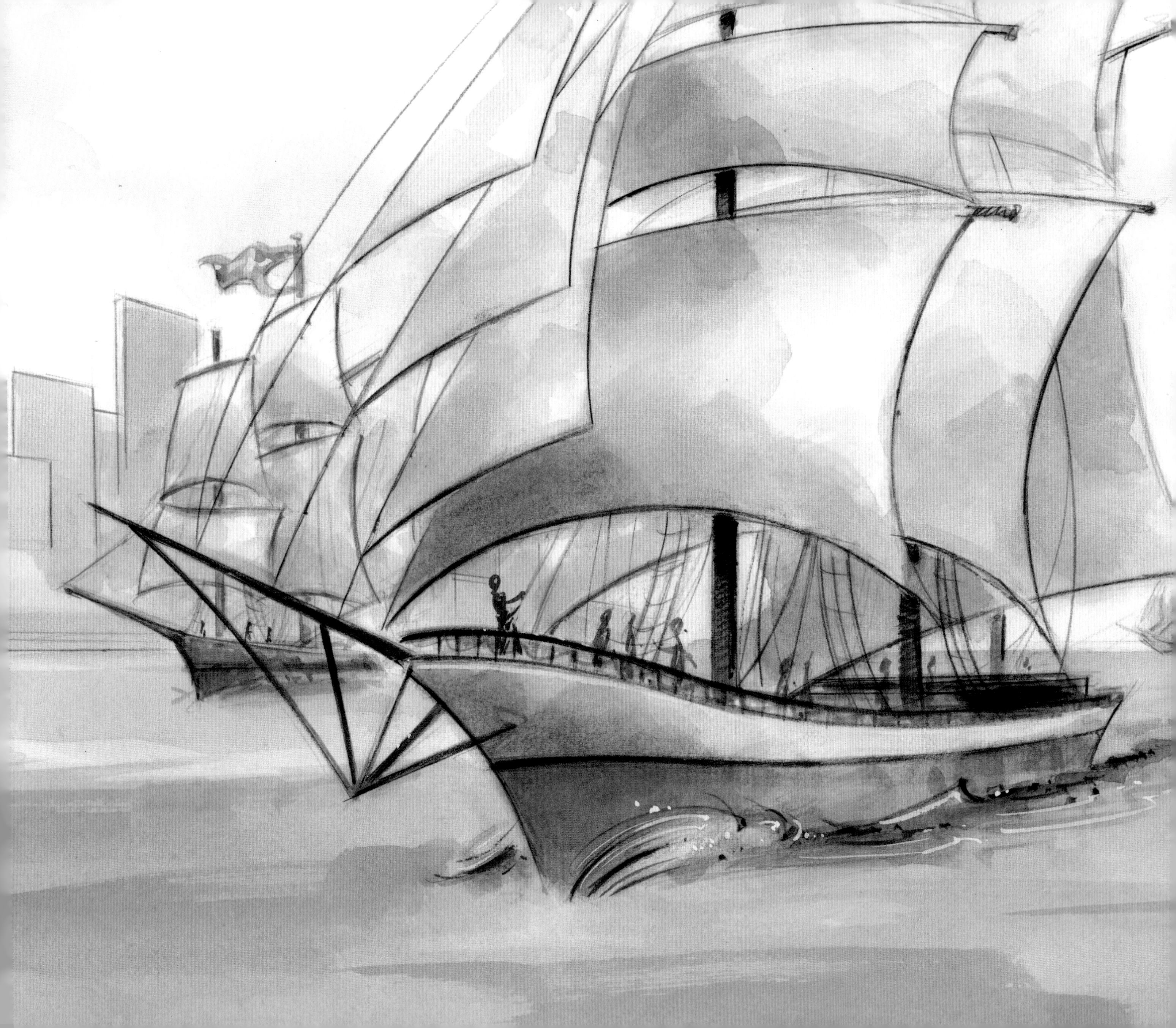

all Ships from all over the world had sailed into New York Harbor before. But this year, there was something special. Something no one had ever seen.

Among the ships was a Viking ship. A Viking ship carrying real Vikings.

There was Thorvald, a great warrior; Helga, the master navigator; and their son, Vigfus, known for his good heart. They had been sailing a long, long time and they were really, really hungry.

"Are you *sure* we're the first ones here?" asked Vigfus, looking around curiously.

But his parents were so dazzled by the new world before them that they didn't even hear him.

"Bag some reindeer!" yelled Thorvald as they leaped off the ship.

"And don't forget to pillage and plunder!" Helga reminded Vigfus sweetly.

Helga didn't find any reindeer, but she did find Danish Modern Furniture.

Thorvald didn't find any reindeer either,
but on Lexington and Twenty-third he was
chased by a very rare breed of moose.

Vigfus had the most success, single-handedly capturing a school bus parked near the American Museum of Natural History. “This is the greatest victory of my life!” he said as he stuffed his sack with lunch boxes. “Tonight we eat string cheese!”

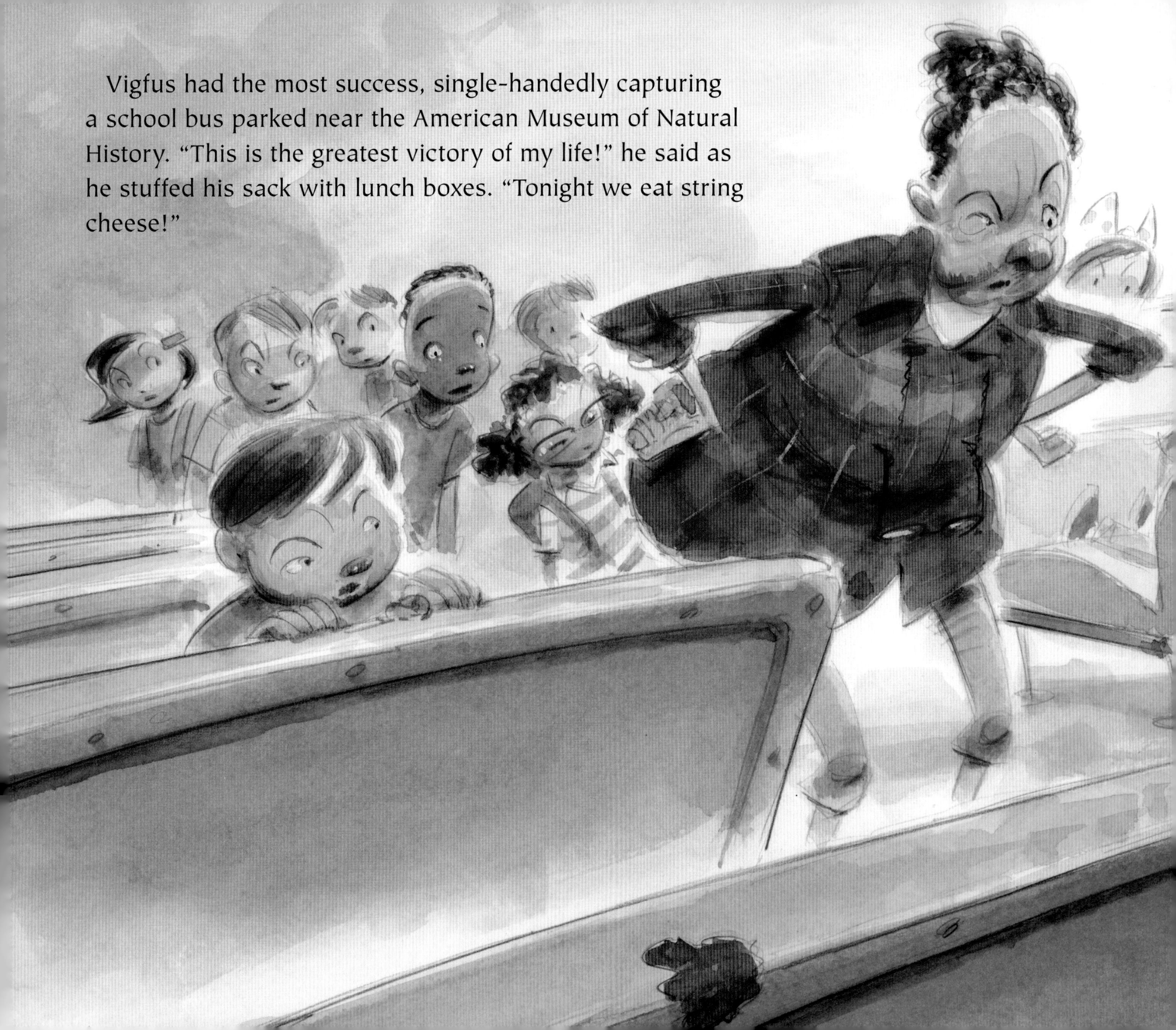

But then the kids of Madison Elementary School came back to their bus and found Vigfus. *Oh no!* thought Vigfus, *I'm severely outnumbered.* To make matters worse, there was a powerful troll blocking his escape. *I'd better just try to blend in,* he thought.

So Vigfus took a seat beside a young mountain shepherdess. She sat very straight and barely looked at him. *It's working!* thought Vigfus. *No one notices me.*

But they did notice him, and he didn't blend in, and he knew that was true when the one they called Bus Monitor gave him a scary look. Immediately he surrendered his crossbow, harpoon, and the coupon for half-price Broadway tickets a warlock had given him in midtown.

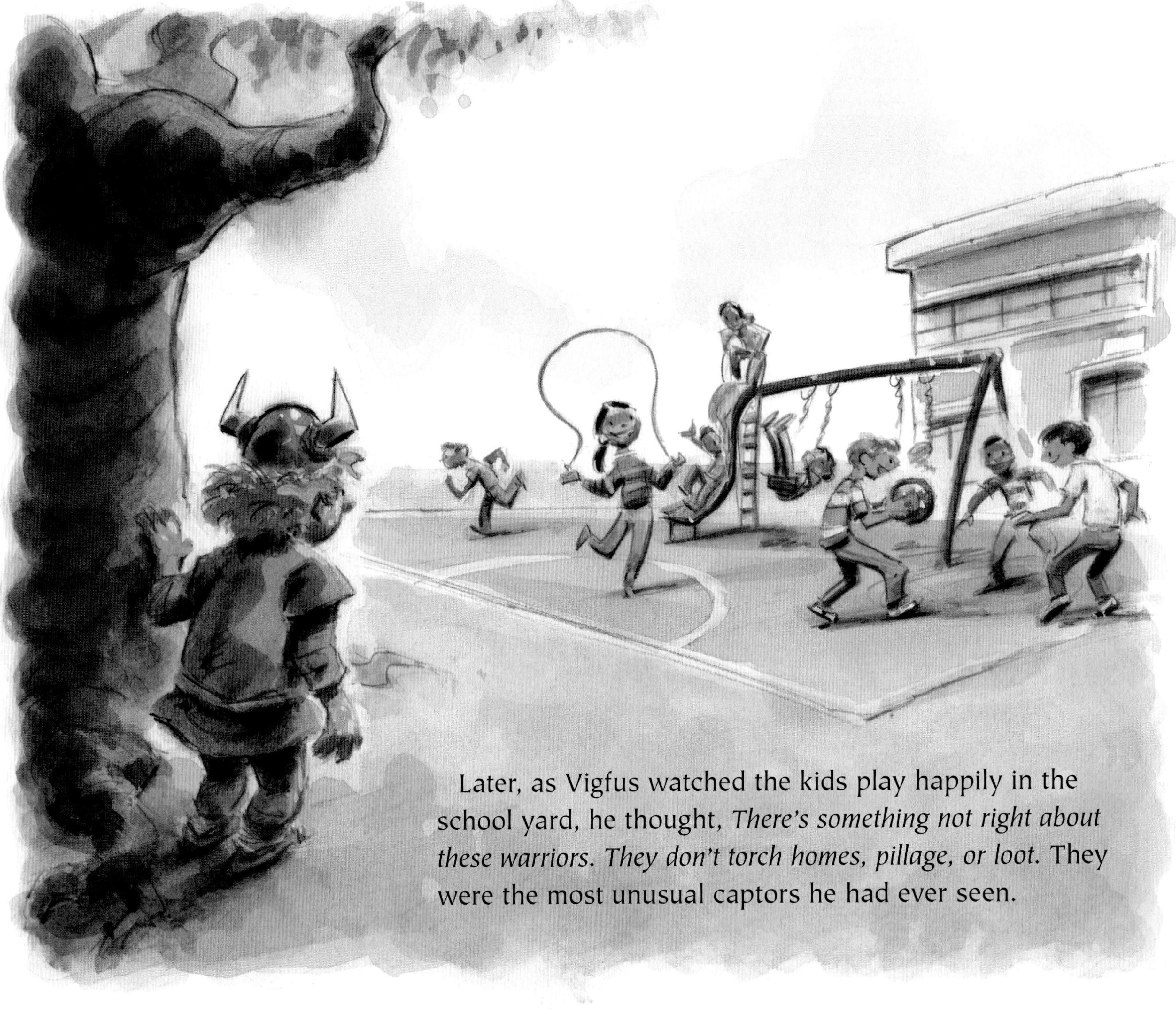

Later, as Vigfus watched the kids play happily in the school yard, he thought, *There's something not right about these warriors. They don't torch homes, pillage, or loot.* They were the most unusual captors he had ever seen.

And then Vigfus saw the strangest thing yet: a boy sharing food. For no reason at all.

"Why did you do that?" asked Vigfus.

"Because he's my friend," said the boy. Suddenly everything made sense. They were all friends. Vigfus had never even heard of friends before. And now, more than anything else in the world, Vigfus wanted to have a friend, too.

But making friends was harder than he realized . . .

especially since no one had told him the secrets.

And Vigfus discovered there were all kinds of secrets, from brushing your teeth, to not picking your nose, to not eating endangered species for lunch.

These non-Vikings had exciting new ideas about everything!

During recess, Vigfus saw someone with a strange helmet and a very skinny club. "At last!" he said. "Another Viking! He'll be my friend for sure." So Vigfus rushed to greet him with the traditional Viking salute.

But it turned out the boy wasn't a Viking. He was Mike, the principal's son. And that's how Thorvald and Helga got called in to see Principal McMullen.

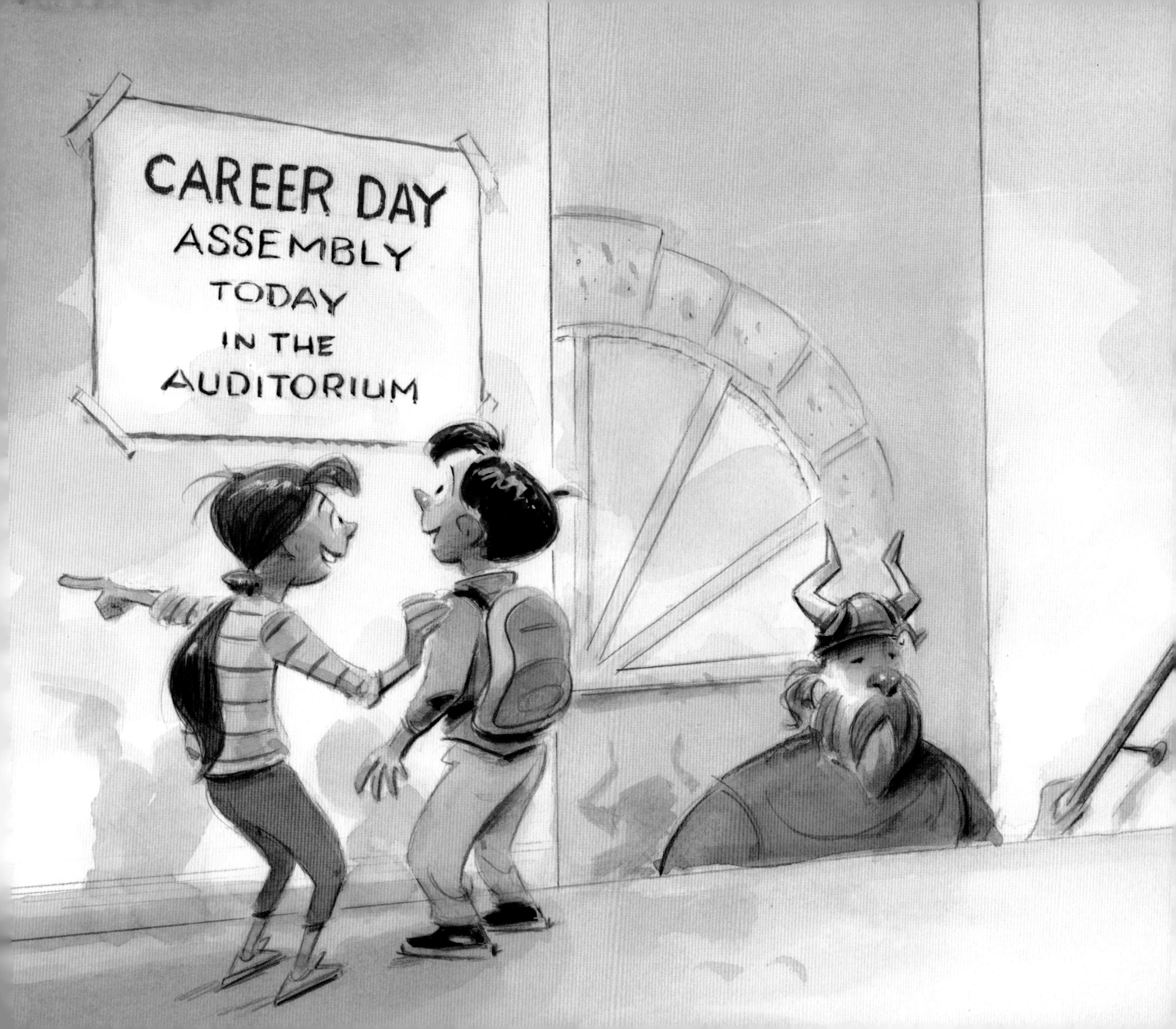
CAREER DAY
ASSEMBLY
TODAY
IN THE
AUDITORIUM

Thorvald and Helga came to school right away. But when they got there, Helga navigated them west instead of east, and they became featured speakers at Career Day.

". . . And not only do we slay sea-serpents, and pickle their insides," Thorvald told the crowd, "but we also get to eat with our hands!"

When the assembly was over, three kids wanted to be policemen, two wanted to be firemen, and 127 wanted to be Vikings.

Finally Thorvald and Helga met with Principal McMullen. They were surprised by his office. Clearly this great ruler had fallen on very hard times. So they did their best to restore the fullness of his glory.

"O mighty King!" said Thorvald. "We pledge you eternal loyalty!"

"And pay you tribute," said Helga, "with a bowl of my famous weasel soup."

"Um, thank you," Principal McMullen replied. "Are you aware that Vigfus skewered another student to a tree?"

"Yes, and we're very proud of him," said Thorvald.

"That student was my son," said the principal.

"Your Majesty's shame is safe with us," said Thorvald.

"While I appreciate that," said Principal McMullen, "there are some important rules that need to be followed. . . ."

Meanwhile, outside the principal's office, Vigfus was worried. He wondered if Mike's father owned a giant whip.

"No," said Mike, "but I saw a movie where they used a giant whip to fight a seven-headed viper."

"*I* used one to fight a seven-headed viper!" said Vigfus.

"Really?" said Mike. "Wow! That is so cool!"

And in that moment, something wonderful happened. Vigfus made his first friend.

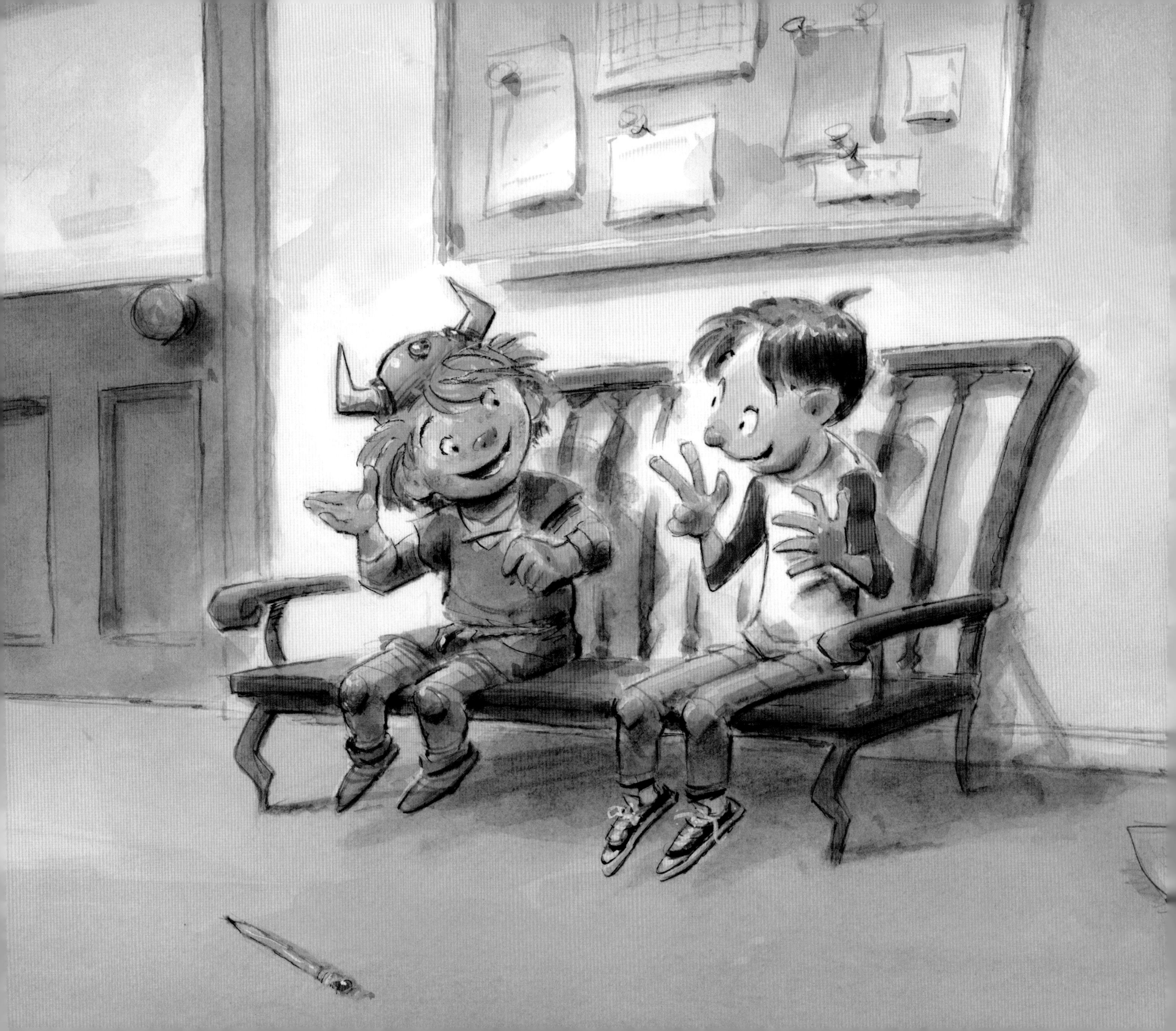

After meeting with the principal, Thorvald wasn't happy about the new rules. "No bullying? No biting? No bonking? Our people have been doing those things for generations!"

"Do we have to return *everything*?" asked Helga.

"Yes," said Vigfus.

"Even the Bellacio espresso maker?" asked Helga.

"Yes," said Vigfus.

"Even Moosey?" asked Thorvald.
"Yes," said Vigfus.
And Moosey agreed.

Vigfus told Thorvald and Helga that they also had to wait their turn in line, say "excuse me," and mop up after their oxen.

"It all seems so very un-Viking," Thorvald grumbled.

"But don't you want to make new friends and be happy?" asked Vigfus.

"I'm not even sure what a friend is," admitted Helga.
So Vigfus tried his best to explain.

"A friend is someone who helps you when you need it. Or who tells you if you have ketchup and bean dip on your nose."

"And if a friend does something that hurts you, he always says, 'I'm sorry.'"

Thorvald and Helga were unsure about the new rules, but they were willing to give them a try.

Over time, Vigfus, Thorvald, and Helga worked hard to fit in and learned how to make many friends. But even so, they felt that something wasn't quite right.

"I miss being a Viking," said Vigfus.
"So do we," said Thorvald and Helga.

Then, on a beautiful day in Central Park, something important occurred to Vigfus. Maybe they didn't have to give up who they were to be happy.

"We can still be Vikings!" exclaimed Vigfus. "We can still torch things, and we can still eat with our hands. Oh, and one more thing . . ."

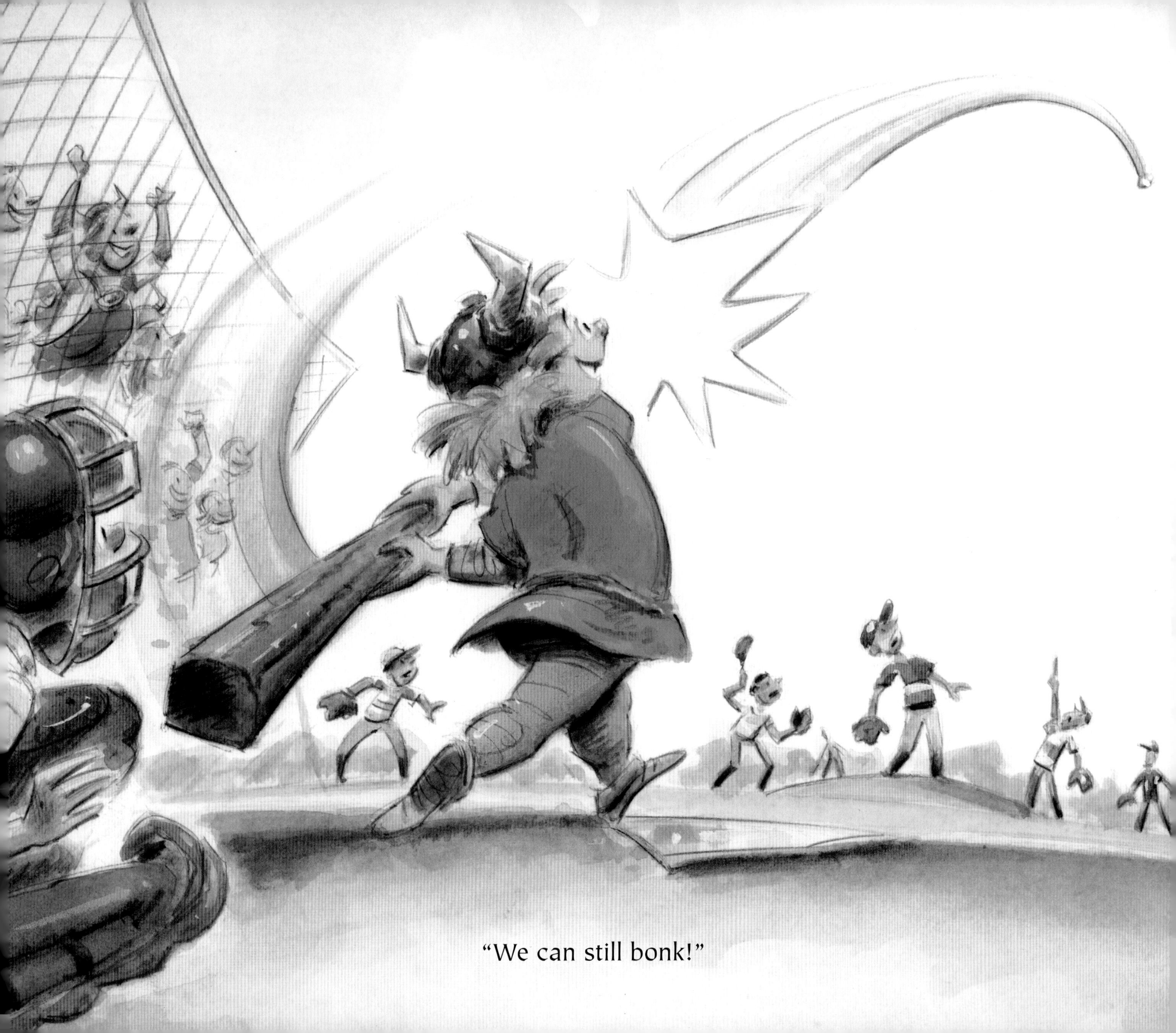

“We can still bonk!”